The Clockmaker of Mullen

Jamison & Esther Escott

Papillon Publishing

Copyright © 2004 Jamison and Esther Escott
All rights reserved.

Published by Papillon Publishing
an imprint of Blue Dolphin Publishing, Inc.

For inquiries or orders, address
Blue Dolphin Publishing, Inc.
P.O. Box 8, Nevada City, CA 95959
Orders: 1-800-643-0765
Web: www.bluedolphinpublishing.com/Papillon/

ISBN: 1-57733-127-3

Library of Congress Cataloging-in-Publication Data

Escott, Jamison, 1966-
    The clockmaker of Mullen / Jamison & Esther Escott.
        p. cm.
Summary: When a plague of rats finally breaks the town clock and stops
time, the clockmaker quietly takes advantage of the situation.
    ISBN 1-57733-127-3 (pbk. : alk. paper)
    [1. Fairy tales. 2. Clocks and watches—Fiction. 3. Rats—Fiction.] I. Escott,
Esther, 1934- ill. II. Title.
    PZ8.E866 C1 2004
    [E]—dc21

                                                                    2002015370

First printing, January 2004

Printed in China

10   9   8   7   6   5   4   3   2   1

eep in the forests of the Old World, nestled beneath high, snow-capped mountains, lay the beautiful village of Mullen. It was a quaint, little town, with cobblestone streets and brightly painted houses. You'd think that the people who lived there would have been happy. But they were not. They seldom heard singing in their village, and they never heard laughter. The people of Mullen were worried and sad.

For years, their village had been plagued by rats. Everywhere people looked, they could see rats darting from one hiding place to another. There were so many rats, and they were so bold, that the cats in town were afraid of them.

The rats got into Baker Karlson's flour, even though he kept it on a shelf high off the floor. They startled

Grandma Elsa's chickens at their feeding trough, where they ate the chickens' grain. Mothers fearfully shook out the bed covers each night before tucking their children in to sleep. On every street, in every attic, in every cellar, rats could be heard scratching and gnawing through day and night.

Near the center of town, an old clockmaker kept his small shop. He was a kind man, and he loved the people of Mullen. Each day at his workbench, while making and repairing clocks, he watched people pass by his front window. It worried him to see how unhappy they looked. As he waved to school children, they would look up and smile, then go on with their faces down again. It seemed to him that even their smiles were sad.

Nobody knew how old the clockmaker was, for he had been tending his shop as long as anyone could remember. Directly above the shop was a one-room apartment in which he lived. Neighbors brought him whatever supplies he needed, and it was generally believed that he had never set foot outside. This may have been true, for on no occasion had anyone ever seen the old clockmaker walking the streets of town.

Above his tiny apartment, in a tower higher than any other building in the village, stood the town clock. The clockmaker himself had built this clock. Every Sunday morning, before having his cup of tea, he climbed the staircase into the tower to wind the spring. He had to do this early in the day to keep the clock running, for by Sunday morning the old spring was nearly run down.

"This may be a day of rest for me, my friend," he would say to the clock as he stood amidst its gears and wheels and turned the heavy crank. "But there is no rest for you!" And so, the clock kept accurate time year after year, and people set their own clocks by its chiming. In fact, because it had kept such perfect time for so very long, some of the older folks in the village believed that the great clock made time itself run.

At the end of each weary day, the old man climbed into his bed below the clock tower. Most nights he would lie awake a while, worrying about the rats and wondering if the people of Mullen would ever be free of them. Then, as he slept, the clock chimed right above him all night long, ringing out the hours, the half hours, and the quarter hours. He had grown so accustomed to the clock's

deep, mellow tones that he slept right through the chiming.

But one Sunday morning just before dawn, when the night was its very darkest, he suddenly awoke. For a moment, he lay staring wide-eyed in the darkness. Then he realized what was wrong. He had awakened because the clock had *not* chimed.

He stepped out of bed and put on his slippers, then pulled a jacket over his nightshirt, for the night air was cold. With a lantern in his hand, he climbed the narrow, winding stairs to the tower above.

The clock's heavy gears were strangely silent and un-moving. He shone his lantern all about the great machine as he searched for the problem. Then he looked up, and there it was. A rat had gotten its tail caught in the gears. It hung there with what seemed an evil gleam in its tiny eyes. But it did not move a whisker. It was frozen in time.

The clockmaker stood there a few seconds, thinking. Then he stepped to the tower window. Peering upward, he noted a wisp of cloud that hung motionless in front of the moon. As he gazed downward, the dark village looked as still as a painting. Nothing moved. Not a single

cricket chirped, and no night breeze stirred the needles of the pines.

At last he returned to the clock, and the dangling rat. "Enough is enough," he said, as he plucked the rat from the gears. The machine remained still, for the spring was too run down to start the massive gears moving again. "Ah, well," he said to the clock, "I suppose you deserve a rest after all." With that, he started down the steps, carrying the lantern in one hand and the motionless rat in the other. Along the way, he stopped to pick up a large, burlap sack and placed the rat inside.

He reached his shop, and opened the front door. He paused, the sack clenched firmly in his fist. Then, dressed in his nightshirt and jacket, he stepped out into the darkness. Something unheard of was happening, and none of the townspeople were awake to see it. The clockmaker, who never traveled outside his shop, was walking the streets of Mullen.

The night was filled with a strange silence, as he placed one foot after another. He stepped softly, but his footsteps sounded loud in the stillness. He turned a corner and came upon the milkman's horse and wagon,

standing like statues in a park. What an odd sight they were! He stared at them a moment, and then moved on. The streets became less familiar, as he walked further from the part of town he saw every day from his shop window.

Then he began to notice the rats. They were everywhere, in the gutters, on the doorsteps, and in the gardens and back alleys. Two of them sat on a rooftop, seeming to leer down at him, as he approached the first house. He knocked on the door, forgetting that the people inside could not answer. "How silly of me," he said aloud, smiling at his mistake as he let himself in.

Ignoring the sleeping people, he moved quickly through each room. He found rats on the table, hunched over crumbs. On the window sill, a rat had been gnawing at the curtains. He found them in all kinds of positions, even scratching themselves. They were bright-eyed and very much alive, but they didn't move a hair. He picked up one, gently studied its long whiskers, then picked up another. At first he smiled as he lifted them by their tails and dropped them into his sack.

But as he moved from house to house, he became more and more disgusted with the rats. He found two of them locked in a bitter fight, and he thought, what nasty little animals! At Baker Karlson's shop he saw a large flour sack badly chewed and spilling out, and he knew that the flour was ruined. He shook his head at such waste, and said aloud, "I must get rid of these terrible creatures!"

He continued searching houses, gathering rats as he went, until after a while the dark, winding streets began to seem very much alike. At one point he became confused when he realized he had entered the same house twice. But he trudged wearily on, trying not to lose his way.

And so it went that the old man searched the entire village, until he had collected every single rat. The task took many hours, and if time had been running, it would

have been late in the afternoon. As it was, except for the bright moon above, the night remained dark.

At last he started down the winding road that led out of town. He had a plan. He would take the rats to the river and throw them in. Dragging the sack, which had become too heavy to carry, he finally reached the bridge over the river and stopped to catch his breath. He decided to open the bag once more to look at the rats.

Inside the sack, they were curled together peacefully, and didn't look like such terrible creatures after all. In fact, they looked surprisingly innocent. The clockmaker realized that, for all the trouble they had caused, the rats hadn't done anything wrong. They were just being rats, doing what rats do.

He glanced over the bridge to the water below. Moonlight shone beautifully on the motionless waves. But he knew that beneath the serene surface the water was deep and dark and cold. He sighed, and muttered wearily, "What in the world am I going to do?"

Then he saw something in the shadows below the bridge. A small boat was tied there, in the weeds along the shore. He left the bridge and made his way carefully down the steep bank to the river, dragging the sack with him.

At the river's edge, he pulled on the rope to bring the boat closer. Struggling with the bag, stumbling once and nearly falling into the water, he finally managed to hoist the heavy sack into the boat. He carefully laid the sack open, so the rats could get out. Then he untied the boat and gave it a mighty shove toward the center of the stream, where it stopped. He knew that if the current were flowing, it would carry the boat far downstream to where the river became shallow and slow. The rats would find a new home there, in forests and grassy meadows.

"Have a safe journey," the clockmaker called out to the rats. Then, climbing up the bank to the bridge, he grumbled, "But don't come back!"

On the long, dark road back to the village, his feet grew heavier with each step. Even the lantern felt heavy. By the time he reached his shop, his legs were wobbly and he could scarcely keep his eyes open. He longed for his bed. But the old man climbed the narrow stairs past his bedroom, up into the tower. There was one more job he had to do.

He reached the gears of the clock and started turning the crank to wind the spring. The clock was completely silent and still and, tired as he was, it took all his strength to start it. The gears lurched heavily, stopped, and then moved again. At last, the great clock was running.

Stepping to the window, he saw that the little cloud which had stopped was moving again, drifting past the moon. Then he heard a horse's hooves clopping on the street below, and looked down to see the milkman's horse and wagon turning the corner. Above the eastern mountains, the sky was beginning to brighten with the first pale glow of dawn.

Just then, the clock began to chime. Loudly and clearly its voice rang out over Mullen, waking the little village from the longest, deepest sleep it had ever known.

As the morning grew brighter, doors and windows all over town flew open and shouts arose. One after another, neighbors called happily to each other. Children ran outside in their nightshirts, shouting in their excitement, "Where did all the rats go?"

The clockmaker stretched and yawned. As he made his way down the stairs to his apartment, he decided not to go back to bed after all. He pulled trousers on over his nightshirt and went down to his shop. On Sundays he never worked, but gave himself a day of peace and rest. So he made his usual cup of tea, opened his window and settled himself at his workbench to watch the children playing in the street.

"Clockmaker! What happened to all the rats?" they called to him through his window. But he just shrugged, as if he were as puzzled as they were. Their joyful faces filled him with contentment, and he smiled and waved to them as he sipped his tea. The clock above him chimed

again, and all through the day it rang out the hours, the half hours, and the quarter hours.

Not a single rat was ever seen again in the village of Mullen, nor did anyone guess the cause of their sudden disappearance. However, those who saw the clockmaker that day thought he looked to be very tired, indeed.

And since time is running even now, the great clock must be working still.

After earning a Bachelor of Arts degree from U.C. Santa Cruz, Jamison Escott traveled the country, spending several years in the eastern United States. He now lives in his native Santa Cruz Mountains with his wife, Kathy, and young son, Charlie, and commutes to the Silicon Valley. He enjoys fixing up the house and teaching his son to skip stones across the river in the backyard.

Esther Escott was born in Pennsylvania, where she taught Art in the public schools. After moving with her husband, Charles, to California, they raised two sons. She collaborated with their younger son, Jamison, by illustrating this story. Esther also enjoys hiking, being a grandmother, and baking blackberry pies.